D1123858

PERFECTLY
Arugula

STERLING and the distinctive Sterling logo are registered
trademarks of Sterling Publishing Co., Inc.

Library of Congress Cataloging-in-Publication Data Available

10 9 8 7 6 5 4 3 2 1

Published by Sterling Publishing Co., Inc.
387 Park Avenue South, New York, NY 10016
Text and Illustrations © 2009 by Sarah Dillard
Distributed in Canada by Sterling Publishing
c/o Canadian Manda Group, 165 Dufferin Street
Toronto, Ontario, Canada M6K 3H6
Distributed in the United Kingdom by GMC Distribution Services
Castle Place, 166 High Street, Lewes, East Sussex, England BN7 1XU
Distributed in Australia by Capricorn Link (Australia) Pty. Ltd.
P.O. Box 704, Windsor, NSW 2756, Australia

Printed in China
All rights reserved

Sterling ISBN 978-1-4027-5954-3

For information about custom editions, special sales,
premium and corporate purchases, please contact
Sterling Special Sales Department at 800-805-5489
or specialsales@sterlingpublishing.com.

The artwork for this book was created using
watercolor, gouache, and colored pencils.
Designed by Lauren Rille and Jessica Dacher

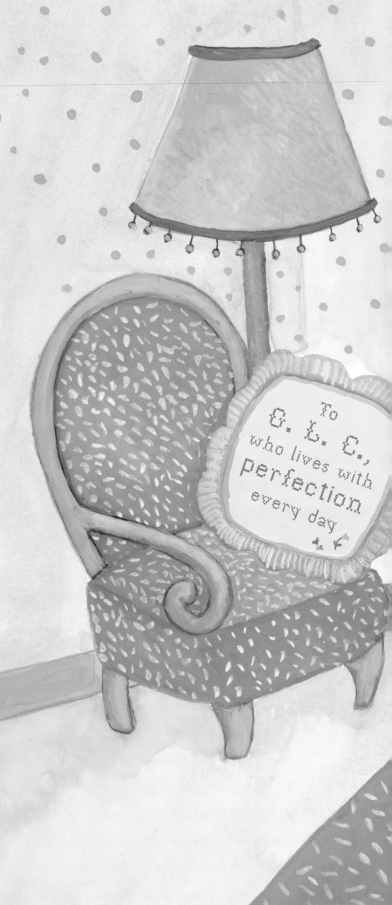

To
G. L. C.,
who lives with
perfection
every day

PERFECTLY Arugula

by Sarah Dillard

PROPERTY OF THE
NATIONAL CITY PUBLIC LIBRARY
1401 NATIONAL CITY BLVD
NATIONAL CITY, CA 91950

Everything in Arugula's world was just so.

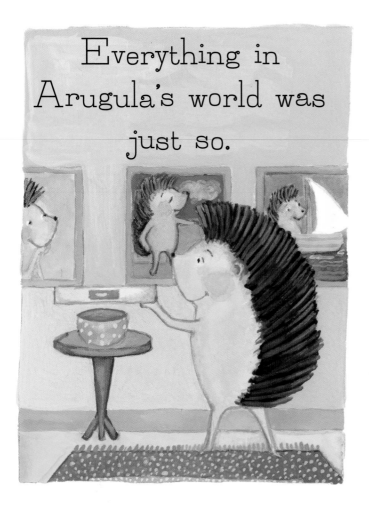

Her house was clean and bright.

There were no weeds in Arugula's garden.

Her quills had just the right shine and bounce.

Arugula

was perfect!

One morning while she was brushing her teeth, Arugula had an idea. She thought about it all day.

I should have a party.

A tea party would be nice.

I'll serve watercress sandwiches.

And cream puffs.

Everything will be just perfect!

The next day, Arugula went shopping for her party.

She invited everyone she saw, except for Fidget.

Before long, the word was out about Arugula's tea party.

Everyone was excited about it.

No one was more excited than Arugula.

Everyone will have a perfectly wonderful time!

Arugula cleaned,

and Arugula cooked.

This should be enough.

That takes the cake!

Oops! Just enough time to freshen up!

Arugula was ready.
Everything was perfect!

One by one, Arugula's guests arrived.

Come in, Pistachio! Don't forget to wipe your feet.

Be careful with that teapot, Basil! It's a valuable antique.

Here's a coaster, Parsley, so you don't leave a ring on the table.

Watch out for crumbs, Pansy! They are so hard to get out of the carpet.

Don't you just love those teacups, Clover? They are very fragile and chip easily.

You'd better let me cut the cake, Forsythia. It is very hard to do neatly.

Come in, Fox! Make sure you latch the door. We don't want to let the cold air in.

Arugula's guests were
perfectly miserable.

Suddenly Fidget burst into the room.

Once Fidget broke the ice, everyone
had a perfectly wonderful time.

Except for Arugula.

Arugula was devastated.

Finally, Arugula's party came to an end. It had indeed been perfect.

Arugula went to work cleaning up.